# Zara Takes Flight

## *A Young Fairy's Journey to Independence*

**Author: Kimberly Sweitzer**

**Illustrator: Jessica McClurg**

*Zara Takes Flight*: A Young Fairy's Journey to Independence

Author: Kimberly Sweitzer

Illustrator: Jessica McClurg

Published by Clever Clowder Press



ISBN: 979-8-836-18954-9

Printed in the United States of America

1st Print Edition

## DEDICATION

I would like to dedicate *Zara Takes Flight* to Southern Garrett High School's Class of 2020, which includes my son, Jake. They survived and thrived during their senior year and I'm so proud of them!

I would also like to dedicate my book to my grandchildren, Lucy and Ryan, who make me laugh, smile, and see the world with such joy and excitement. You are loved so very much, and I know that God has great plans for you!

*"For I know the plans I have for you," declares the Lord, "plans to prosper you and not to harm you, plans to give you hope and a future."*

*(Jeremiah 29:11)*

# Acknowledgments

First and foremost, I thank God for giving me the insight, inspiration, and ideas to create *Zara Takes Flight*. He showed me that although things were quite a *mess* in 2020, it could be turned into a *message* of hope to share with others.

I would also like to express my sincerest gratitude to Jessica McClurg. As the illustrator, she shared her time, artistic talent, and imagination, which truly captured who Zara is.

Finally, I would like to thank my family and friends who encouraged me to write my first book. A special thanks goes to my husband, Bob, and my friend, Rhonda, for their love and support. I would also like to thank John McLaughlin, my friend and mentor, for helping with edits and insight.

Today began her journey to the land beyond the trees.
Zara was a bit nervous, but this new life she must seize.
She was ready to make a change and travel to her new home,
to meet other young fairies and hoped to never feel alone.

As she set out on her trip and soared through the sky, she could tell by the clouds that a storm was nearby. The sky began to darken and huge, dark clouds rolled out. "Should I continue my flight?" she thought, as she began to pout.

A fierce wind then blew, causing her to quickly spiral down.
Lower and lower to the earth her tiny body was bound.
She hit the surface hard and cried in pain with a shout.
Her journey would be postponed, she knew without a doubt.

Zara lay there with injured wings and a body that was bruised.
This was not supposed to happen! She was utterly confused.
As the wind and rain hurled against this dainty, young sprite,
she knew she needed shelter from her unexpected plight.

With her magic sparkle gone, and darkness all around,
the only way to see was to feel along the ground.
Through the muddy grass, she finally felt a hole.
"Into the earth it is. Underground I must go."

Slowly Zara crawled into the tunnel and to her surprise, her sparkle came back and she could see what lay before her eyes. Hundreds of tiny creatures, as tiny as she, stared at her and wondered, "Just what could she be?"

They each had six legs, two eyes, and two antennae.
Their bodies were strong and the color of burnt sienna.
Their kindly, wise leader stepped forward and said,
"Child, do not fear us. You have nothing to dread."

"We will protect you so you can heal and find rest.
Being kind to others is the thing we do best.
Now settle in and dry off; some food you must need.
Make yourself at home; please accept our good deed."

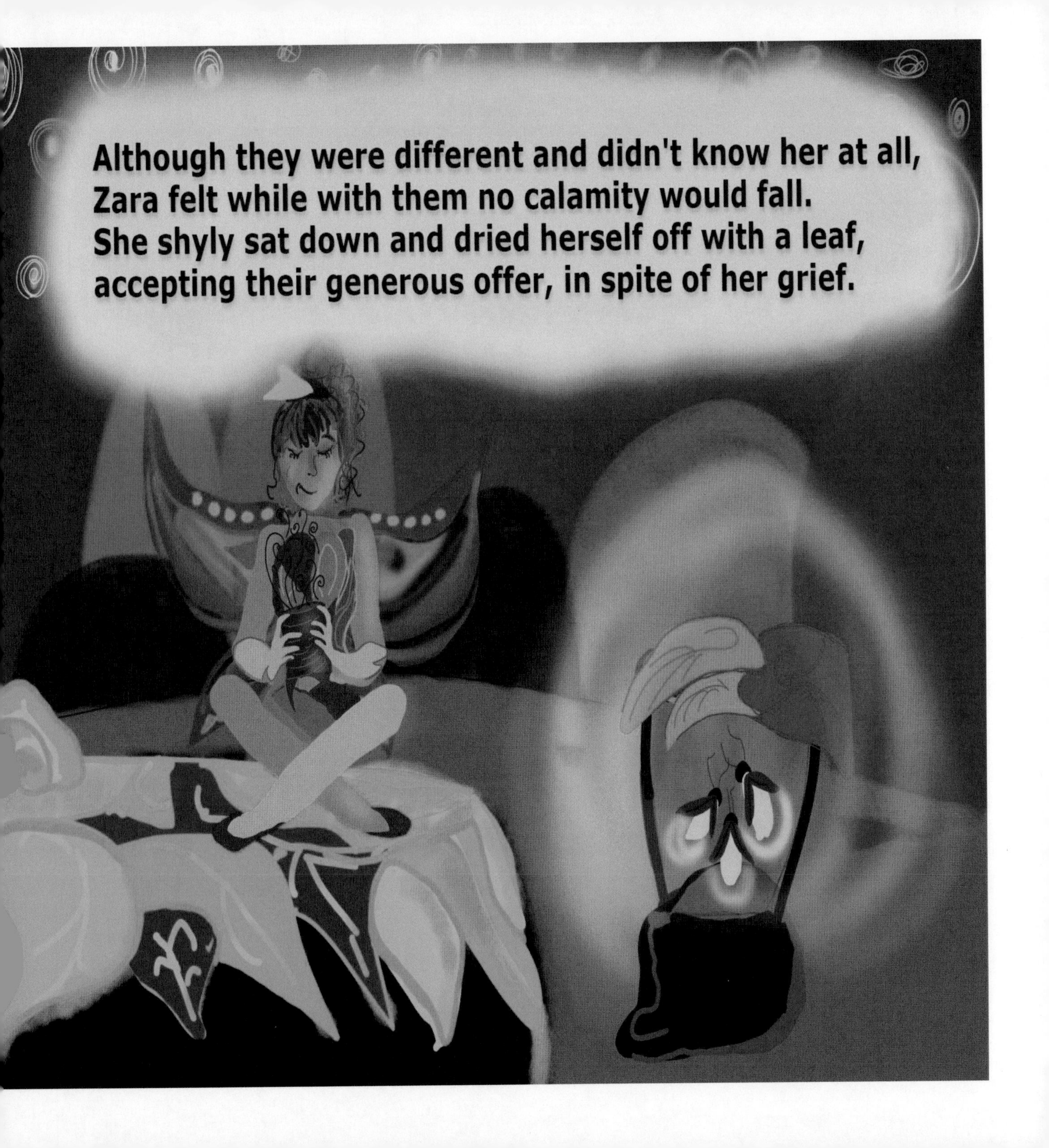
Although they were different and didn't know her at all,
Zara felt while with them no calamity would fall.
She shyly sat down and dried herself off with a leaf,
accepting their generous offer, in spite of her grief.

**Zara was offered nectar, honeydew, and seeds; oranges, corn, mushrooms, and lots of green leaves. She could see that they wanted to be kind and so caring. It was obvious by the food and their dwelling they were sharing.**

The kind creatures went happily back to their labor,
but their leader stayed with Zara to be a good neighbor.
He asked if she needed anything before he left. She said
"No, but thank you, kind Sir, for sharing your nest."

With her belly plenty full and feeling rather safe, Zara decided to rest in this cozy, little place. She was sore and very tired, so she decided to slumber. To sleep she fell quickly, feeling secure and unencumbered.

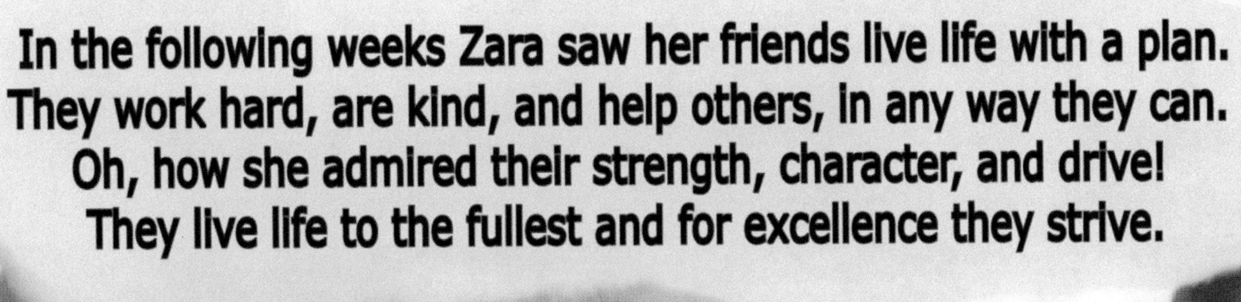

In the following weeks Zara saw her friends live life with a plan.
They work hard, are kind, and help others, in any way they can.
Oh, how she admired their strength, character, and drive!
They live life to the fullest and for excellence they strive.

They work together as a team to complete their many tasks.
Never do they boast or brag, for in humility they bask.
When one of them is in trouble, they arrive by their side.
offering help and support; never being cruel or snide.

In the daytime they lovingly care for their young, and don't rest or frolic until their work is all done. They are always prepared for the winter and snow, so hunger is a misfortune they will never undergo.

**Zara was very content being accepted by her new tribe. She had healed, been fed, and rested, but it was now time to decide. Should she stay where it's comfortable, yet not be able to fly? Or should she take flight into the wide-open sky?**

The wise leader looked at Zara as he looked at one of his own. "My child, I am proud of you; you have learned and you have grown. You know how to work and be part of something great, but staying with us any longer is not meant to be your fate."

"You have been given many gifts to share with the world.
They cannot be used here, in a tunnel to be unfurled!
Your wings are now strong and you are ready to fly.
This was your resting place; now you must take to the sky."

"Take the lessons we have taught you wherever you go.
We love you and will miss you more than you'll know.
You are an amazing creation; a true one of a kind.
Go out and use your gifts to help all of humankind."

Zara thanked her colony and knew what she had to do; continue her journey, no matter what hardships may ensue. She was now much more confident that she was in control. She had learned to believe in herself and listen to her soul.

As she flew to her destiny she felt grateful for her friends. Although she left the tunnel this is not how her story ends. Zara lived life to the fullest; she did more than just survive. She used and shared her gifts with others; Zara learned how to thrive.

Through life she followed the lessons she learned while underground. She taught them to her children; it was the best advice to be found. Be kind, never give up, and always do your part. These things Zara learned from her colony, and they were always with her in her heart.

## About the Author/Illustrator

Kimberly Sweitzer is a Spanish teacher, wife, mother, grandmother, and crazy cat lady. She has always enjoyed writing as a way of expressing herself and was inspired to write Zara's story in 2020 to instill hope during times of adversity. This is her first published book but plans to write more in the future. When not spending time with her family and friends, she loves traveling and using her artistic abilities to sing, paint, and write.

Jessica McClurg strives every day to create unique art that elicits all types of emotions. She grew up in Western Maryland, right on the border of West Virginia, spending most of her time outdoors. Her favorite place to be, to this day, is outside with her easel and oil paints. She has been creating for as long as she can remember, and is inspired by flowers, music, and acts of kindness.

Made in the USA
Middletown, DE
28 June 2022